AaBb Cc Dd Ee Ff Gg Hh Ii Jj Kk Ll Mm

nOoPpQqRrSsTtUuVvWwXxYyZz

For my goddaughters Michaela and Julianna

ANN ESTELLE STORIES

Queen of the CLASS

BY MARY ENGELBREIT

HarperCollinsPublishers

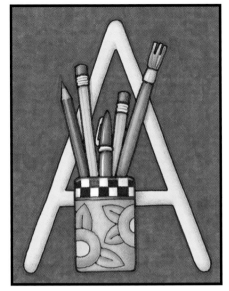

nn Estelle's class was putting on a play. They needed someone to play a king, someone to play a princess, and several people to play a dragon—and they needed someone to play the Queen.

Ann Estelle felt she would be *perfect for the part.* She already had a long red velvet robe and a glittery golden crown, just in case something like this ever came up.

AaBbCcDdEeFfGgHhIiJjKk

Ann Estelle practiced her *queenly manners* at home and at school. "May I have some orange juice, forsooth?" she asked her father.

" Nn Oo Pp Qq Rr Ss Tt Uu

ueens do *not* clean their rooms," she announced regally.

"Then I don't think I'll see a Queen getting Pizza with us tonight," replied her mother.

"Well," Ann Estelle admitted, "I haven't exactly gotten the part yet. . . ."

Cc Dd Ee Ff Gg Hh Ii Jj Kk

Finally the day came when Ann Estelle's teacher, Mrs. McGilligan, announced the parts. Michael was the king. Sophie was the princess who fought the dragon. Harry, Will, and Hannah would play the dragon.

"And the part of the Queen goes to . . . ," Mrs. McGilligan began.

Ann Estelle sat up very straight and imagined *a crown* on her head.

"... Josephine Dolittle!"

Ann Estelle could **not** believe Josephine would wear the long red robe and the glittery crown.

Josephine would be the Queen, and Ann Estelle would be . . . the **Stage manager.**

C c D d E e F f G g H h I i J j K k

Ann Estelle didn't even know what a stage manager was.

"You're very important," Mrs. McGilligan explained. "You'll open the curtain and make sure the actors have what they need.

"I picked you to be the stage manager, Ann Estelle, because I know you're very clever and responsible."

Ann Estelle did not want to be responsible. She wanted to be Queen.

A ll week long the actors practiced their parts. Michael had the very first line in the play. "A terrible fate has befallen my kingdom!" He had a lot of trouble remembering it, so Ann Estelle had to help him.

As a matter of fact, Ann Estelle had to learn everybody's lines so that she would know when to open and close the curtain, and when to change the scenery. She was **very busy.**

Ann Estelle got all the costumes ready. The princess's sword was just plain wood. Ann Estelle thought it would look better covered with *shiny aluminum foil.* She fixed a big rip in the king's cloak with Mrs. McGilligan's stapler. She even figured out a way to make it look like there were flames shooting out of the dragon's mouth.

When no one was looking, she tried on the Queen's crown.

It fit perfectly, of course.

Ann Estelle **sighed.**

Everyone's family came to see the play. Ann Estelle pulled the *curtain* back at just the right moment.

Michael was standing in the middle of the stage. He stared at all the people in the audience. He swallowed. He didn't say a word.

"A terrible fate has befallen my kingdom!" Ann Estelle whispered as loud as she could.

"A terrible fate has befallen my kingdom!" Michael said.

And the play went on.

Ann Estelle watched from backstage as the princess went bravely forth to fight the dragon. "Grrr! Grrr! ROAR!" yelled Harry, Will, and Hannah. Ann Estelle looked down at the table next to her. She gasped. Sophie had forgotten her sword!

Ann Estelle thought fast. She grabbed the sword from the table. She picked up a cardboard shield so she would look like a soldier. Then she ran out onto the stage.

"Y our highness!" she said. "Here is your **Sword!**"

She bowed to Sophie and ran back off the stage.

And the play went on.

Sophie defeated the *dragon,* who roared and fell on the floor. The Queen returned to her kingdom in her golden chariot.

The play ended, and Ann Estelle pulled the curtain closed at just the right moment. Then she pulled it open again so everyone could take **a bow.**

The audience clapped and clapped. "We want the stage manager!" Mrs. McGilligan gave her a little push onto the stage.

Ll Mm Nn Oo Pp Qq Rr Ss Tt Uu

Ann Estelle stood up very straight. She felt just like **a Queen.**

AaBbCcDdEeFfGgHhIiJjKkLlMm

Queen of the Class
Copyright © 2004 by M. E. Enterprises, Inc.
Manufactured in China. All rights reserved.
www.harpercollinschildrens.com

Library of Congress Cataloging-in-Publication Data
Engelbreit, Mary.
Queen of the class / by Mary Engelbreit.
p.   cm. — (Ann Estelle stories)
Summary: Ann Estelle feels she
would be perfect to play the role of the
queen in the class play.
ISBN-10: 0-06-008178-3 (trade bdg.)
ISBN-13: 978-0-06-008178-2 (trade bdg.)
ISBN-10: 0-06-008179-1 (lib. bdg.)
ISBN-13: 978-0-06-008179-9 (lib. bdg.)
ISBN-10: 0-06-008180-5 (pbk.)
ISBN-13: 978-0-06-008180-5 (pbk.)
[1. Kings, queens, rulers, etc.—
Fiction. 2. Theater—Fiction.
3. Schools—Fiction.] I. Title.
PZ7.E69975 Qu 2004
[E]—dc21
2002152094   CIP
AC

Typography by Stephanie Bart-Horvath
❖
First Edition

nOoPpQqRrSsTtUuVvWwXxYyZz